ADDY'S LITTLE BROTHER

ADDY · 1864

BY CONNIE PORTER
ILLUSTRATIONS GABRIELA DELLOSSO
AND DAHL TAYLOR
VIGNETTES SUSAN MCALILEY

THE AMERICAN GIRLS COLLECTION®

Published by Pleasant Company Publications
Previously published in *American Girl®* magazine
© Copyright 2000 by Pleasant Company
For information, address: Book Editor, Pleasant Company Publications,
8400 Fairway Place, P.O. Box 620998, Middleton, WI 53562.

Printed in Singapore.
00 01 02 03 04 05 06 07 TWP 10 9 8 7 6 5 4 3 2 1

The American Girls Collection® and logo, American Girls Short Stories™,
the American Girl logo, Addy®, and Addy Walker®
are trademarks of Pleasant Company.

Edited by Nancy Holyoke and Michelle Jones
Designed by Laura Moberly and Kimberly Strother
Art Directed by Julie Mierkiewicz and Kimberly Strother

Library of Congress Cataloging-in-Publication Data

Porter, Connie Rose, 1959-
Addy's little brother / by Connie Porter ;
illustrations, Gabriela Dellosso and Dahl Taylor ; vignettes, Susan McAliley.
p.   cm. — (The American girls collection)
Summary: After her brother joins the family in Philadelphia at the end of
the Civil War, Addy wants to be with him as much as possible, so she is
jealous when he starts spending time with her friend's cousin. Includes
information about the life of African Americans in Philadelphia
in the late 1860s and a recipe for letter cookies.
ISBN 1-58485-033-7
1. Afro-Americans Juvenile fiction. [1. Afro-Americans Fiction.
2. Brothers and sisters Fiction. 3. Jealousy Fiction.]
I. Dellosso, Gabriela, ill. II. Taylor, Dahl, ill. III. Title. IV. Series.
PZ7.P825 Adc 2000 [Fic]—dc21   99-38622 CIP

The
AMERICAN GIRLS
COLLECTION

OTHER AMERICAN GIRLS
SHORT STORIES:

FELICITY'S DANCING SHOES

AGAIN, JOSEFINA!

KIRSTEN AND THE NEW GIRL

SAMANTHA SAVES THE WEDDING

MOLLY AND THE MOVIE STAR

PICTURE CREDITS

The following organizations have generously given permission to reprint illustrations contained in "Looking Back": p. 36—Photographs and Prints Division, Schomburg Center for Research in Black Culture, The New York Public Library, Astor, Lenox and Tilden Foundations; p. 37—illustration by Laszlo Kubinyi; The Library Company of Philadelphia; p. 38—illustration by Laszlo Kubinyi; p. 40—Chester County Historical Society, West Chester, PA; p. 42—Abraham Lincoln by Peter Baumgras, McLellan Lincoln Collection; Brown University Library; p. 44—Photography by Jamie Young, Prop Styling by Jean doPico.

TABLE OF CONTENTS

ADDY'S FAMILY

POPPA
Addy's father, whose dream gives the family strength.

MOMMA
Addy's mother, whose love helps the family survive.

ADDY
A courageous girl, smart and strong, growing up during the Civil War.

SAM
*Addy's sixteen-year-old
brother, determined to
be free.*

ESTHER
*Addy's two-year-old
sister.*

SARAH MOORE
Addy's good friend.

ADDY'S
LITTLE BROTHER

Riddle me this, Addy," said Sam. "Where the only place it make sense to put a cart before a horse?"

Addy loved trying to guess her brother's riddles. It was a game they played often. "I know it ain't a stable. How about a unstable?" Addy asked.

Sam laughed. "That's pretty clever," he said. "But the place where *cart* go before *horse* is the dictionary."

"That's a good one, Sam," Addy said.

Addy held her brother's hand, doing her best to keep up with his long-legged stride. It was a dreary Sunday with clouds low in the sky, but Addy was happy. Sam was walking her to her friend Sarah's.

"Can we go to the candy store?" Addy asked. "I was hoping I could get some black licorice to share with Sarah."

Sam said, "Maybe later. I'm going to drop you off and go home to rest awhile. I'll come back for you."

"You really that tired?" Addy asked.

Sam let out a whistle. "Girl, you never worked stables. The boss have you doing two, three things at once. Mucking, harnessing, cleaning cabs. He need more workers."

Addy was happy. Sam was walking her to her friend Sarah's.

Addy asked, "Why don't he hire more?"

"He cheap. He rather wear us out," Sam said. "I don't know about that sociable on Saturday. After working all week and then a half day Saturday, I might be too tired to go."

Addy stopped. "Sam, you *promised*. A sociable ain't sociable if you by yourself."

church

"You wouldn't be by yourself. The church is going to be full up with giggling little girls."

Addy giggled despite herself. "That ain't true. All the youth groups coming." She smiled at her

4

brother. Sam had been separated from the family for over a year, fighting for the Union during the war. He'd lost an arm in battle. Addy had worried about him so. Even a walk to a friend's house with Sam seemed special.

The hall in Sarah's building was long and dark, and the family's room steamy and filled with laundry. "Hey, y'all," Sarah said when she opened the door. Two irons sat on top of the stove, and near the stove stood a tall, thin boy Addy had never seen before. "Addy, Sam, this here is my cousin Daniel," Sarah said.

"Hey, Daniel," said Addy. Daniel

nodded once, then turned away. *That's rude,* Addy thought, but Sarah didn't seem to notice.

"I got some crackling," said Sarah. "We can eat it while we study."

"That sound good," Addy said. Ever since Sarah had quit school to work, Addy had been helping her with her studies. Today Addy had spelling and arithmetic for Sarah to work on. As the girls settled in at the table, Sam went to speak to Daniel. Daniel didn't say much, but he smiled. Then Sam looked up and said, "Me and Daniel going out."

"I thought you was going home to rest," Addy said.

"I changed my mind," said Sam.

"We going to the park to play marbles. Daniel will like that better than sitting around with two girls."

"What's wrong with that?" asked Addy. "*You* sit around with two girls all the time. Me and Esther." Esther was Sam and Addy's little sister.

Sam rubbed his hand over Addy's head. "That's why we leaving," he said, grinning.

Addy didn't think Sam's joke was very funny but soon forgot all about it. The girls ate crisp bits of crackling, dipping the fried pork skin in peppery vinegar, and Sarah did her arithmetic. She also told Addy about Daniel. He was 12. His mother and father had been born in slavery but escaped to Canada, where Daniel was born. After the war, the family moved back to America. They had been in Philadelphia for less than a week.

"This the first time we all been together," Sarah said. "My momma and Aunt Eva talk all night. Sometimes they cry, but mostly they laugh and tell me to go to sleep. But I can't because I'm so happy. I know Daniel is, too. He just don't show it. He real quiet."

Addy recalled how she'd felt about the noise and rush of big-city life when she first came to Philadelphia. Maybe Daniel was just shy.

When they finished the schoolwork,

Sam and Daniel still hadn't come back. Addy was worried. She and Sam would be expected back for supper soon. So she said good-bye to Sarah and went to the park.

A group of boys were gathered in a clearing. Sam was kneeling at the edge of a huge circle drawn in the dirt. He had a marble in his hand, and marbles were scattered all over the circle.

"This here is going to be number seven," Sam said. He took aim, knocked a marble out of the circle, and yelled, "Ringer!"

Some boys groaned, but most cheered, and Addy cheered with them. Daniel knelt beside Sam, and Addy felt

a little jealous as she pushed her way through the crowd. "Bye, Sam," Daniel was saying as she reached them. "Thanks for the cat's-eye."

"A cat's-eye?" Addy asked as Daniel headed off for home. "That some kind of riddle?"

"It's some kind of marble," Sam said.

"I bought it for him. I'm taking Daniel to the stables tomorrow, too. The boss is sure to hire him since he won't have to pay him much."

Addy and Sam walked on. When they got to the candy store, Sam kept going. "Ain't we supposed to be getting candy?" Addy asked.

Sam said, "We ain't got time to stop now."

Addy didn't say anything. She kicked hard at a clump of dirt and thought jealously, *You had time to stop and get Daniel a marble.*

☀

Daniel was hired at the stables, and

Sam began training him, so on Monday and Tuesday he missed supper. Addy missed having Sam at the table. Sam always had a story to tell, and after supper they would sometimes play mancala. Esther would think she was playing, too, and scoop up beans from the board. Addy would talk about her day, and Sam always listened.

mancala

When Sam came to supper on Wednesday, he told plenty of stories, but they were all about Daniel. Daniel learned quickly, and the boss liked him. Daniel could polish the leather harnesses until they were soft and shiny. He could carry two buckets of water that weighed

12

twenty pounds each. He didn't flinch when a mouse jumped out of the oat bin and ran up his jacket sleeve. Daniel wasn't afraid of Thunder and Lightning, the draft horses, even though Lightning was mean and had nipped him.

Poppa said, "Sound like the boy don't know fear."

Sam said, "He can even answer my riddles."

"Maybe Daniel is the little brother you always wanted," Poppa said.

Addy put her fork down. "I never knew you wanted a brother," she said to Sam.

"I did," said Sam. "When you was born, I wanted Momma to take you back to the cabbage patch and bring a boy instead."

Momma said, "Sam, stop kidding your sister. Addy, when you was born, Sam acted like you was his baby. He carried you around like you was a doll. Esther, too."

"Esther, too," Esther repeated. Everyone laughed but Addy. She could remember when Esther was born. They had all fussed over her. They still did. Esther could walk and talk and liked to tag along after Addy, but Addy still saw her as being a little baby. Sam was so much older than Addy was. Addy wondered if Sam saw *her* as being a baby, too.

Sam sure doesn't see Daniel that way, Addy thought glumly. He bragged about Daniel. Maybe Sam really *did* wish he could send her back and get a brother.

Two nights later, when Sam was late again, Addy helped fix him a plate of food. As much as she loved bread pudding, she saved her piece for Sam. She wanted to spend some time alone with him. Addy had a new riddle, one she had heard at recess: *What animal walks on four legs in the morning, two legs in the afternoon, and three legs at night?* She hadn't guessed the answer, and she didn't think Sam would be able to, either.

Sam mussed Addy's hair when he

came in. "What you doing up, girl?" he asked.

"Waiting to see you," Addy said. She got Sam his food while he slipped off his jacket. Then she asked him the riddle.

"Man," Sam said. "He crawl as a baby, walk when he grown, and use a cane when he old. That's a real old one. I asked Daniel it. He thought on it and got the right answer."

Addy folded her arms across her chest. "I don't want to talk about Daniel."

Sam started eating the bread pudding. "Why not?" he asked.

"I just don't," answered Addy, "and

I hope you ain't ask Daniel to go with us to the sociable tomorrow."

Sam wiped his mouth. "I'm glad you brung it up," he said. "I been so busy, I ain't had time to tell you. I ain't going."

A hot streak of anger shot through Addy. "Why not?"

"Don't be mad," said Sam. "You can still go. Poppa will see to you getting home. Most guys my age at church is going to a 'Old Bowler' marbles match over at the park."

"You taking Daniel to it?" asked Addy loudly.

Sam was silent. Then he nodded.

Addy jumped up from her chair. "I'm sick of Daniel and you, too. You *my* brother, not his!"

"Wait now, Addy. Let me explain," Sam said. But she pushed him away and ran up the stairs.

Addy threw herself down on her pallet and pulled the covers over her head. Silent tears ran down her face. Once, back on the plantation, Sam had told her that some folks said that if a girl could kiss her own elbow, she would become a boy. Addy didn't want to be a boy, but she'd tried it anyway, just to see if there was magic in what Sam said. No matter how she'd twisted her arm, she couldn't get her mouth near her elbow. Now, remembering that night, Addy pulled an arm close and tight and tried

*Addy pulled an arm close and tight and tried one more time
to give her elbow a kiss.*

one more time to give her elbow a kiss.

☀

The next morning, Momma fixed Addy's hair for the sociable, tying the braids together with a new ribbon. Addy wasn't feeling very sociable. If she stayed at home, though, Momma would want to know why, so Addy went on to the church by herself. On the way, she passed by the stables and saw Daniel. He was leading

 a team of horses out to a cab.

"Hey, Addy. Hey!" Daniel called out to her.

"Hay is for horses," Addy said sharply, and she kept walking.

She was halfway up the block when Daniel caught up to her. He was covered in dirt from head to toe and smelled foul like the stables. "Addy, do you know where Sam is?" Daniel asked. He seemed nervous.

"Why you want to know?" Addy asked. She knew that Sam was home getting cleaned up to go to the marbles match, but she didn't feel like telling Daniel anything about him.

"If you see Sam, tell him we sure need his help," Daniel replied. "The boss say a man ordered three carriages for a wedding, but the man come in and ask for eight. We got to get the extra cabs ready right away. We're even using

21

Thunder and Lightning. Sam usually handle Lightning, but I'll do it today, I guess."

Addy was thinking ahead. "I guess you ain't going with Sam, then," she said.

Daniel said, "Guess not," and took off.

Addy hurried home. Now maybe Sam could go to the sociable with her! Halfway there, she met Sam, striding up the street.

She ran to him, out of breath. "I saw Daniel, and he said he can't get off work," she said.

"I don't know why he ain't finished," Sam replied. "When I left, all he had to do was water the horses."

Addy avoided Sam's eyes. "Could you go to the sociable with me now? We ain't got to stay the whole time if you don't like it."

Sam put his arm around Addy's shoulder. "All right," he said. "I was going more for Daniel than for myself, anyway. I wanted to apologize last night, but you took off like a scared rabbit. If I'd known the sociable meant so much to you, I wouldn't have backed out."

"It mean a lot, and then again it don't," said Addy. "I been wanting to go so I could do something with you. I like doing things with you, Sam."

"I like doing things with you, too," Sam said.

"Then why you put Daniel ahead of me? I'm your sister," said Addy.

Sam stopped. "Let me explain something about Daniel."

Addy rolled her eyes.

"You brung him up, and you going to hear what I got to say," Sam insisted. He sat down with Addy on a brownstone stoop.

"It ain't that I'm putting Daniel first.

He need somebody to talk to," Sam said. He let out a sigh. "Daniel's brother Quincy was about my age when he was killed in the war. He had joined the Union army. His body was never brung home."

24

Addy felt a chill go through her. She looked at the empty sleeve of Sam's jacket. If Sam had been killed . . . Addy couldn't even think about life without Sam.

"Sarah never told me," she said.

"The family don't like to talk about Quincy much," said Sam. "Daniel miss his big brother. I think he need me."

Addy remembered Daniel's anxious face. Softly, she said, "I think he need you right now." Sam just nodded. Addy went on, speaking fast. "Sam, Daniel said they was in a mess at the stables. They got to get a bunch of coaches ready. They got to hitch up Thunder and Lightning."

"What!" said Sam, leaping to his feet. "I hope Daniel ain't foolish enough to think he can handle those two. Come on!"

Back at the stables, workers rushed about their tasks. Men, wet and speckled with mud, cleaned out carriages while others harnessed and hitched nervous, snorting horses. "We could use a hand here, Sam," said a man nearby.

Sam scanned the yard for Daniel. A driver sped past out of the wide stable doors. Then a piercing whinny came from inside the stables. Addy turned and saw a huge stallion rearing in the dim light, its reins flying loose in the air. Beside it was a small figure—Daniel.

"Sam, look!" yelled Addy.

Sam was at the door in seconds. "Daniel, stop!" Sam called. "Back away from Lightning."

Addy's heart raced. Lightning looked as if he could strike like lightning, quick and deadly. Daniel had backed the horse into a corner and was trying to grab the

reins. Lightning snorted and bucked.
Daniel backed up and fell.

Sam walked slowly forward. "Easy,
Lightning, easy," he said. The horse
pawed the air. Sam kept talking until he
was right beside the horse. Then he
slowly helped Daniel up and moved the
boy behind him. Addy's throat tightened
as Sam reached for the reins. But the
horse stood still and let Sam lead him
peaceably away.

Daniel went to clean up at the pump
as Addy sat, breathing hard, flooded
with relief. If Daniel had been hurt, it
would've been her fault. The sociable
wasn't so important now.

A few minutes later Sam came over.

"That old Lightning anxious to get dressed up and go trotting off to a wedding," he said.

Addy laughed. "Go on with Daniel to the marbles match," she said, picking a bit of hay from her brother's hair.

"You just saying that because I'm a sight," said Sam.

"No, I want you to go. Daniel need you," said Addy. She looked over to where Daniel stood, pouring water over his head. "Maybe Daniel will be like a brother to you someday."

"Maybe," said Sam. "You think of Sarah like a sister. Do that make you think less of Esther or me?"

"No!" Addy insisted. "I don't

know what I would've done without Sarah when me and Momma got to Philadelphia, but I never wanted her to take the place of you or Esther."

"She helped you, and you help her," Sam said. "I'm helping Daniel. But no matter what, I would never want to trade you in for a brother. I need you and Esther. I need my sisters."

Addy gave Sam a hug as Daniel came over, soaking wet. "I don't know what happened," he said. "I thought I could handle Lightning."

"Maybe someday," said Sam. "But in the meantime, stay away from Thunder and Lightning, or at least from their *reins*."

Addy and Daniel groaned at Sam's pun.

Sam said, "Y'all think you can do better?"

Addy took Daniel's hand. They went over to some bales of hay, whispering. When they came back, Addy asked, "Why was the little tree sad its first spring?"

Sam thought. Then he said, "I don't know."

Addy answered, "Because the big tree said it was time to leave."

Daniel said, "Wait, there's more. The little tree said, 'I hate to go now. I'm just putting down roots.'"

Sam threw his head back and

laughed. "Uh-oh," he said. "I'm in trouble with the two of you working as a team."

Addy and Daniel looked at each other and smiled.

CONNIE PORTER

At 9   Now

When I was a girl, I sometimes felt left out when my older brothers made plans with other boys. Over the years, I learned that my brothers' friends might come and go, but I would always be their sister.

Connie Porter is the author of the Addy books in The American Girls Collection.

LOOKING
BACK
1864

A Peek Into
the Past

**CHURCHES
IN
1864**

When Addy was growing up, the
church was the center of Philadelphia's
African American community.

Families came to church
to worship, but many
churches also served as
schools and places for
both political and social
gatherings.

*Mother Bethel Church
in Philadelphia*

In most African American churches,
there were three services every Sunday
and each service was two hours long.
Often, the services ran overtime because
everyone enjoyed celebrating their faith

through prayer and music. Anyone who wanted to could take part in the service. If you felt like crying, or laughing, or clapping to the music, you could. And everyone raised their voices together to sing *spirituals*, or religious songs created by enslaved African Americans.

Many children also attended Sunday school, where they learned Bible stories. During the week adults

During the service, if people felt like answering the reverend, they could.

attended prayer meetings. Some black churches established schools that taught both children and adults reading, writing, and arithmetic. Church leaders knew

 that education was one thing that would help their community's children succeed.

During the Civil War, many churches started freedmen's funds. They collected money for soldiers wounded in the war and for families separated by slavery. In Philadelphia, African Americans organized more than 100 aid societies that helped thousands of people. They gave clothes, food, shelter, and jobs to newly freed people to help them start new lives. For many who arrived in freedom scared and alone, church members were like family.

Families like Addy's also hosted potluck suppers to welcome newcomers. Each family prepared food and brought it to the Sunday meetings. They brought their favorites such as hush puppies, collard greens, and potato salad. Home-made ice cream was a special treat.

hush puppies

One girl remembered that if she worked hard turning the handle of the ice cream freezer, she was given a sweet reward: licking the beater after the cream froze.

Black churches held political events and *abolitionist,* or anti-slavery, meetings. Abolitionist leaders, like Frederick Douglass, gave fiery speeches in black churches. The churches also formed societies to help blacks strengthen the bonds of their own community. Many of the societies had names that connected with

their African heritage, such as the Daughters of Ethiopia or the Sons of Africa.

Church members also gathered together for socials and

Frederick Douglass

fairs. Most often the socials and fairs raised money for the freedmen's funds. Such gatherings were a time for food and friendship. Sometimes the children played games like marbles, Blindman's Buff, or Hot Boiled Beans, or the church's musical or drama group performed.

Some of the fairs were huge events that lasted for days. Great halls were elaborately decorated with banners and flags. Sometimes circuses and concert bands put on free performances, or ministers or abolitionists gave speeches. At the Philadelphia fair of 1864, the

President Abraham Lincoln

main speaker was President Lincoln himself.

The church fair was an exciting event for girls like Addy because they were able to help out. Girls made fruit preserves, helped collect money at booths, or performed in concerts or plays with their Sunday school class.

All of the things that were sold at the fair were made or grown by church members. At the many fair booths, church members sold ice cream, lemonade, candies, preserves, clothing, books, and many other items. Sometimes the women sold their quilts in raffles. One of the most popular quilt patterns was called Jacob's Ladder. Quilts with this pattern were hung outside houses as a signal to escaping slaves that the house was a safe place to stop. These quilts helped escaping slaves reach their own "heaven"—freedom in the North, where they would be welcomed into a church community as if they were family.

Jacob's Ladder quilt

AN
AMERICAN
GIRLS
PASTIME

MAKE LETTER COOKIES

Share a special treat.

Addy and her family spent much of
their free time at the church or helping
freed slaves find food, clothing, or
shelter. Addy wanted Sam to go to the
church sociable with her because it was
important that she be with her family
and friends. Addy might have made her
special letter cookies for the sociable.

Invite your family and friends to a
potluck dinner. Ask everyone to prepare
a special dish to share. Then make these
cookies to share with everyone.

YOU WILL NEED:

An adult to help you

Ingredients

Flour

1 stick premade cookie dough

Butter or margarine to grease cookie sheets

Equipment

Butter knife

Rolling pin

Cookie sheets

Wax paper to grease cookie sheets

Spatula

1. Sprinkle flour on your work surface. Slice off a handful of dough, roll it into a ball, and place the ball in the center of your work surface. Sprinkle flour on top of the dough.

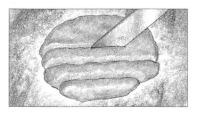

2. Roll the dough until it is about ¼ inch thick. Cut the dough into flat strips with the butter knife.

3. Use the strips to shape the letters. What can you spell?

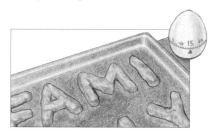

4. Grease the cookie sheets. Place the letter cookies on the sheets, at least 1/2 inch apart. Follow the directions on the cookie dough package for baking.